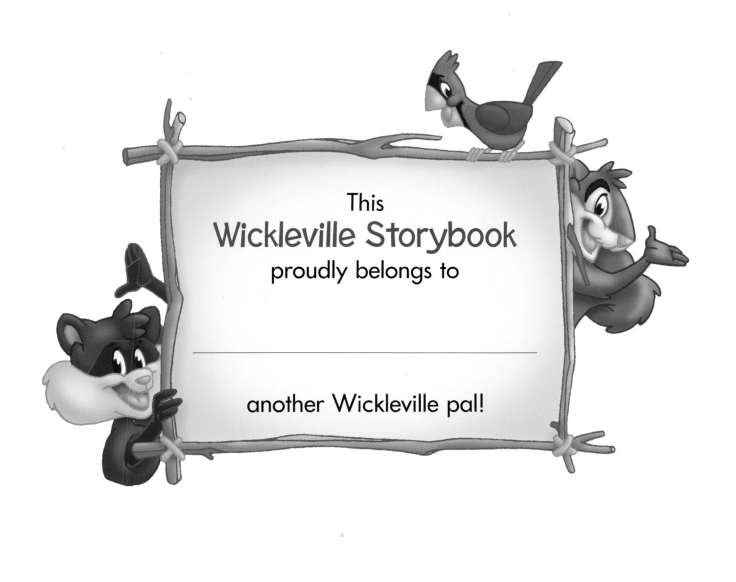

This
Wickleville Storybook
proudly belongs to

_____

another Wickleville pal!

Lynae Wingate, John R. Kober – Editors

Library of Congress Catalog Card Number: 99-69471

ISBN 1-889319-70-8

10 9 8 7 6 5 4 3 2

The Wickleville Woods Pond

by Jeffrey Sculthorp

Illustrations by Lorin Walter

WICKLEVILLE WOODS

TREND enterprises, Inc.

At the edge of the beautiful woods in Wickleville,

a large pond stretches along at the foot of the hill.

Croak found room to play there; it has all that he needs—

3

lily pads, old tree logs, and a whole bunch of reeds.

Happily Croak plays at this end of the pond,

splashing in clean water, of which he is fond.

Suddenly Croak is startled, he wonders what to do.

In the thick reeds he finds garbage and other junk, too!

There's a barrel of green gunk, plus bottles and cans.

Here's a pile of tires and some old beat up fans.

There are garbage bags filled with leaves, twigs, and dirt;

some old pants,
old shoes,
and a
very odd shirt.

Here comes Alpha Bee, just buzzing along,

looking for pollen and singing a song.

14

"What's wrong Croak?" Alpha asked with concern.

15

With a huge frown, Croak said in return...

"I need help cleaning up all of this gunk,

17

all of the litter and all of the junk."

"I'll help you Croak, and ask our friends to lend a hand.

We'll clean up the litter from the pond and the land."

20

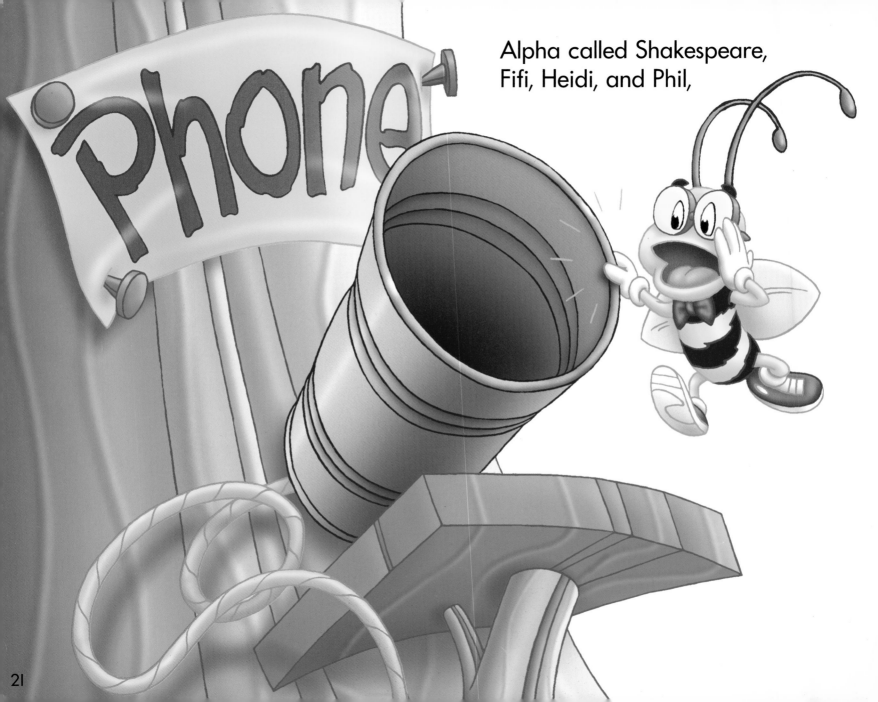

Alpha called Shakespeare,
Fifi, Heidi, and Phil,

to clean up the pond at the foot of the hill.

Shakespeare filled up recycling bags with bottles and cans.

While Heidi and Phil took care of the clothes and the fans.

Fifi and Croak scooped the green gunk away.

Cleaning up all this goop took most of the day.

They all cleaned together, and now Croak can jump,

into a safe, clean pond instead of a dump.